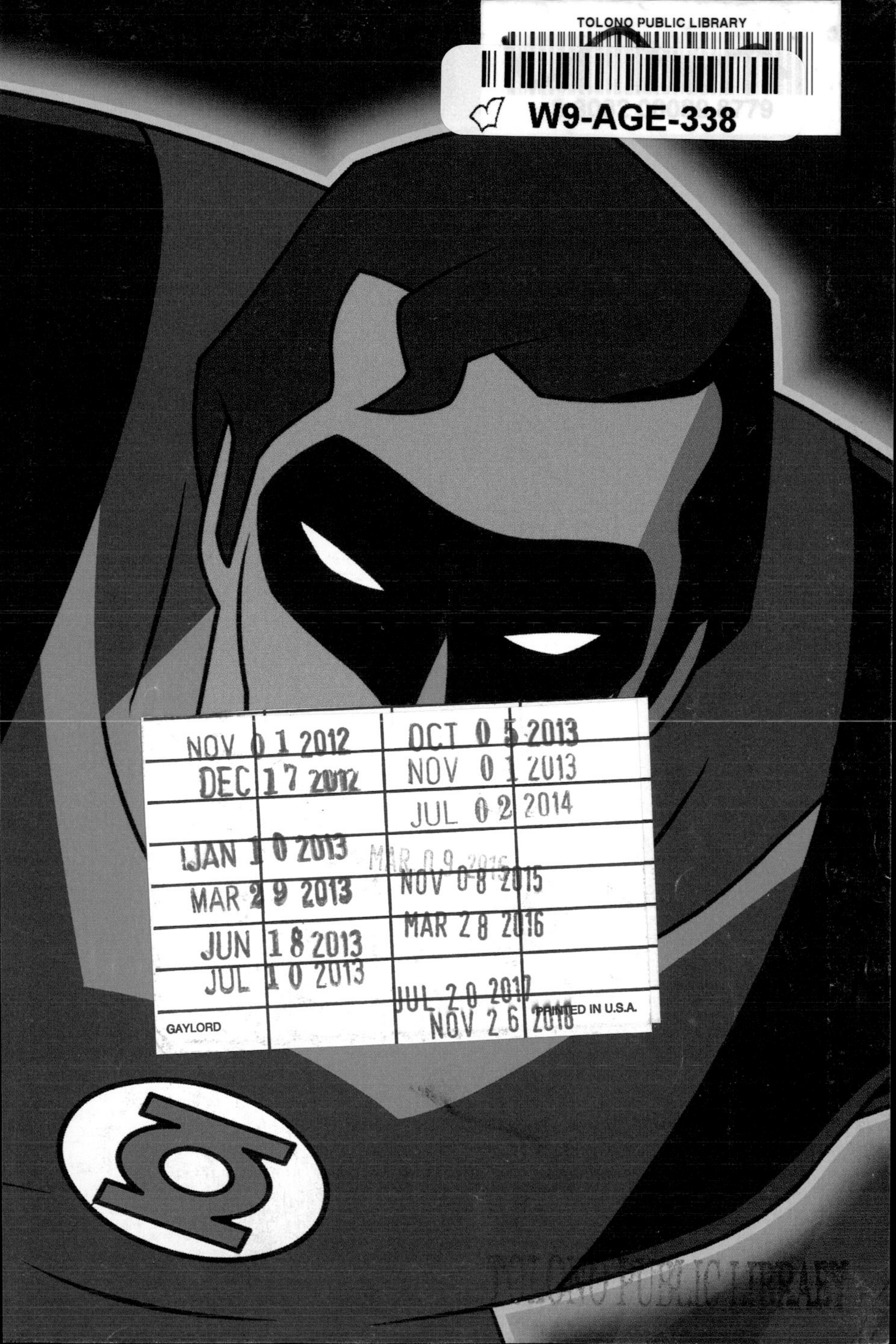

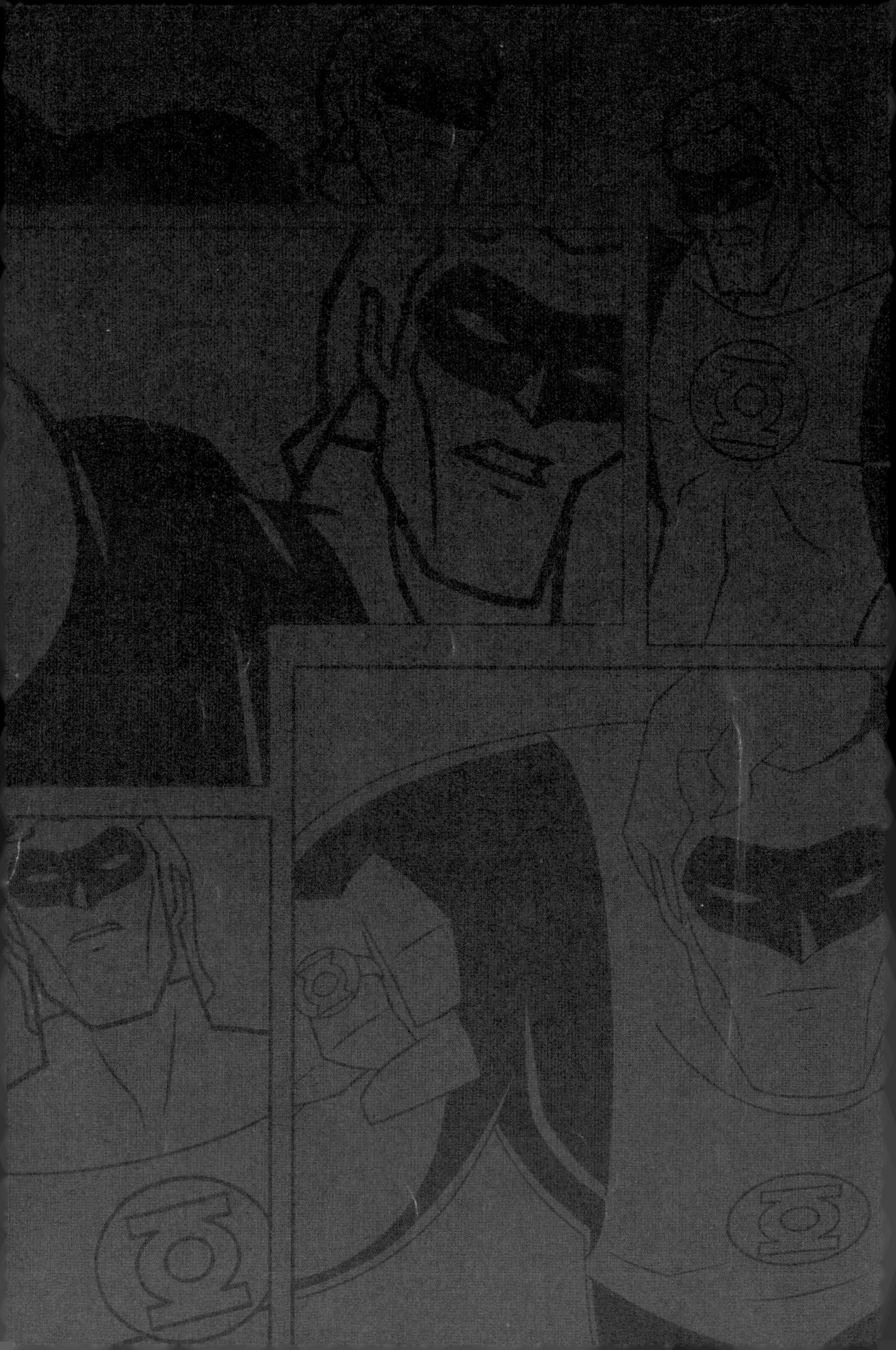

AS THE NEWEST MEMBER OF AN INTERGALACTIC PEACEKEEPING FORCE KNOWN AS THE GREEN LANTERN CORPS, HAL JORDAN FIGHTS EVIL AND PROUDLY WEARS THE UNIFORM AND RING OF . . .

SUPER DC HEROES

GREEN LANTERN

BEWARE OUR POWER!

WRITTEN BY
SCOTT SONNEBORN

ILLUSTRATED BY
DAN SCHOENING

STONE ARCH BOOKS
a capstone imprint

Published by Stone Arch Books in 2011
A Capstone Imprint
151 Good Counsel Drive, P.O. Box 669
Mankato, Minnesota 56002
www.capstonepub.com

Library of Congress Cataloging-in-Publication Data

Sonneborn, Scott.
Beware our power! / written by Scott Sonneborn ; illustrated by Dan
Schoening.
p. cm. -- (DC super heroes. Green Lantern)
ISBN 978-1-4342-2607-5 (library binding) -- ISBN 978-1-4342-3086-7 (pbk.)
1. Graphic novels. [1. Graphic novels. 2. Superheroes--Fiction.] I. Schoening,
Dan, ill. II. Title.
PZ7.S646Bew 2011
741.5'973--dc22   2010025595

Summary: Evil Star and his army are on the loose! Luckily, Hal Jordan, the
Green Lantern of Sector 2814, is hot on their trail. As Hal prepares to attack,
a second Green Lantern shows up from Sector 2815. At first, Hal is grateful
for the help, but Arisia doesn't share the feeling. She's a veteran member of the
Green Lantern Corps and immediately takes charge. If the two can't cooperate,
this super-hero duo will become a dynamic disaster.

Art Director: Bob Lentz
Designer: Hilary Wacholz
Production Specialist: Michelle Biedscheid

Printed in the United States of America in Stevens Point, Wisconsin.
092010
005934WZS11

TABLE OF CONTENTS

CHAPTER 1

FLYING BLIND

Deep in space, a small planet called Porto Collis revolved around its hot, blue sun. Its surface was covered with shiny, silvery-white oceans. The planet was otherwise empty, except for an army of robot guardians the size of battleships.

Today, however, Porto Collis had an unexpected guest. The visitor wore a strange mask shaped like a star and a glowing metal band on his right wrist.

He wasn't there to visit the planet. He was there to rob it!

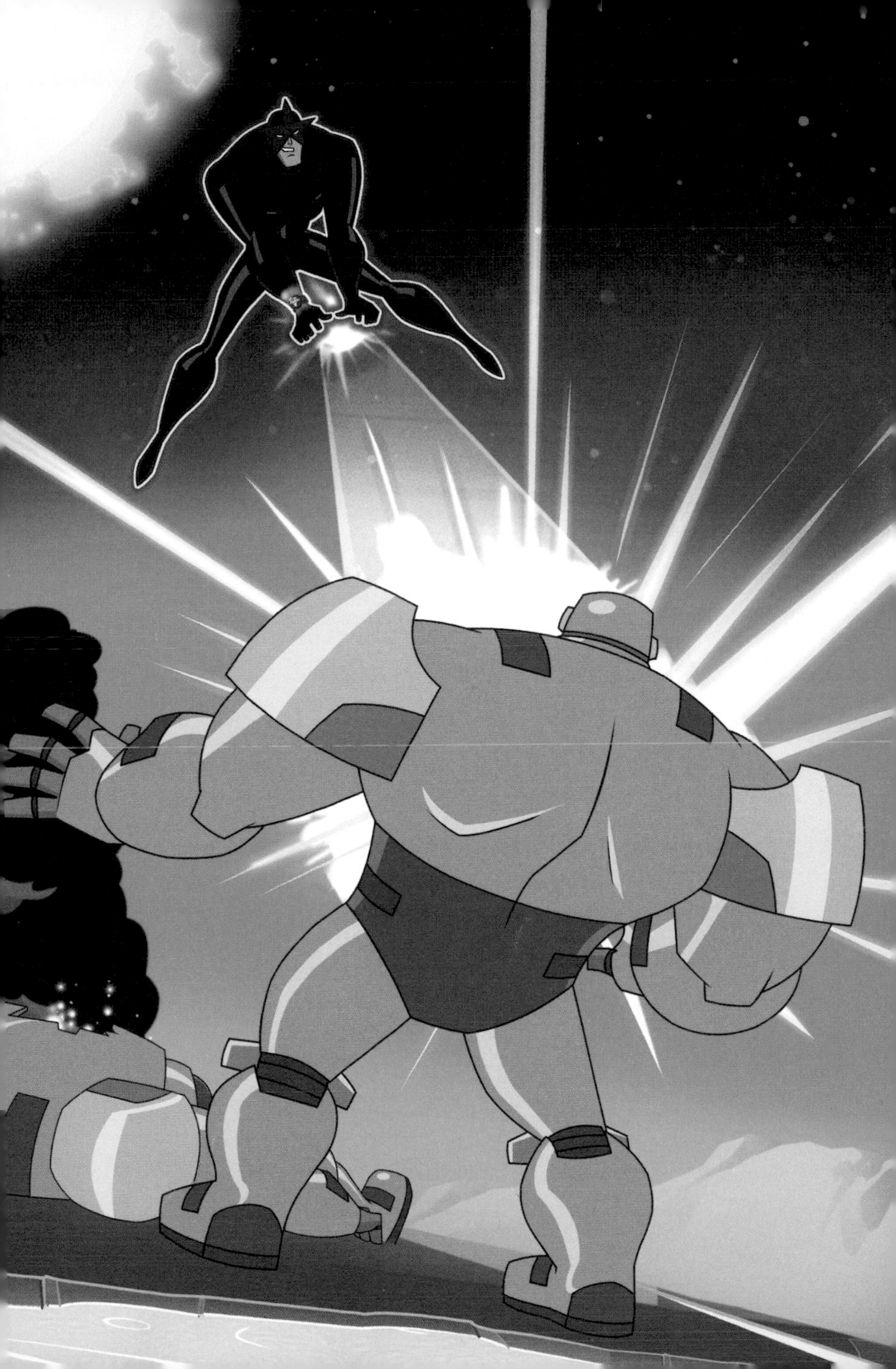

As the alien visitor zoomed down to the planet, the giant robot guards fired their cannons. **BOOM!** It was one man against a hundred cannons. Of course, the battle was over in seconds. As the smoke cleared, it was obvious who had won.

The robot guards were in pieces. The man in the star-shaped mask just smiled.

*   *   *

Back on Earth, Hal Jordan flew through the clouds in the cockpit of a brand new experimental airplane. The sky thundered as the plane flew at the speed of sound
Suddenly, the plane shook as the guidance system exploded. Smoke filled the cockpit. Hal couldn't see out the windows, and he didn't have the computer to guide him. He was flying blind.

Wind whipped past the cockpit as the plane zoomed down. Hal smiled. *No one's ever landed a plane without being able to see,* he thought. *But it's my job to do things that no one's ever done before!*

SKKREEEEEE Hal stopped the plane inches from a hangar. One more second and it would have crashed.

As Hal leaped out of the cockpit, Dr. Kistler, the man in charge of the project, stormed up. "You broke every rule in the book!" he roared.

Hal shrugged with a smile. "It was either break the rules or break the plane!"

Dr. Kistler knew Hal was right, but that only made him madder. He was about to tell Hal how angry he was, when the green ring Hal wore on his hand began to glow.

Hal covered the ring quickly. "Excuse me," Hal told the scientist. "I have to take a call." Hal hurried toward the hangar.

"Call? What call?" asked the scientist. "I didn't even hear a phone ringing!"

Hal ducked out of sight behind the hangar. He looked over his shoulder to make sure no one could see him. *After that landing, Dr. Kistler already thinks I'm crazy,* Hal said to himself. *If he saw me talking to a ring, he'd be sure of it!*

But Hal Jordan was far more than just a test pilot. He was also a member of the Green Lantern Corps. Each Green Lantern was assigned to protect a sector of space. It was Hal's responsibility to defend Earth and thousands of other planets in Sector 2814.

"Okay, what's up?" Hal asked his ring.

"A planet in Sector 2814 is under attack," Hal's ring said. It projected an image of the super-powered thief in a red, star-shaped mask destroying the robot guards on Porto Collis.

"Why would someone want to attack *that* planet?" Hal asked.

"The Outer Space Banking System stores its platinum reserves on Porto Collis," the ring informed him. Platinum was one of the most valuable metals in the galaxy. It was worth more than gold. A *lot* more.

Hal told his ring to transform his flight suit into his Green Lantern outfit. Then he leaped up into the air! "There's only one thing more fun than flying a plane," he said, soaring through the clouds. "And that's flying *without* one!"

A Green Lantern's ring was one of the most powerful weapons anywhere. It let its wearer fly, and it could create anything Hal imagined. It also connected him to the Book of Oa — the history and rules of the Green Lantern Corps — as well as every known fact about the entire galaxy.

The ring continued to tell Hal more. "Porto Collis is on the very edge of Space Sector 2814. It spends half its time in your sector, and half its time in Sector 2815."

"Is there any information on the man in the star-shaped mask?" Hal asked.

"There are no entries that match the attacker's description," replied the ring.

That means I have no idea what I'm going to be facing, thought Hal grimly.

Once again, Hal would be flying blind.

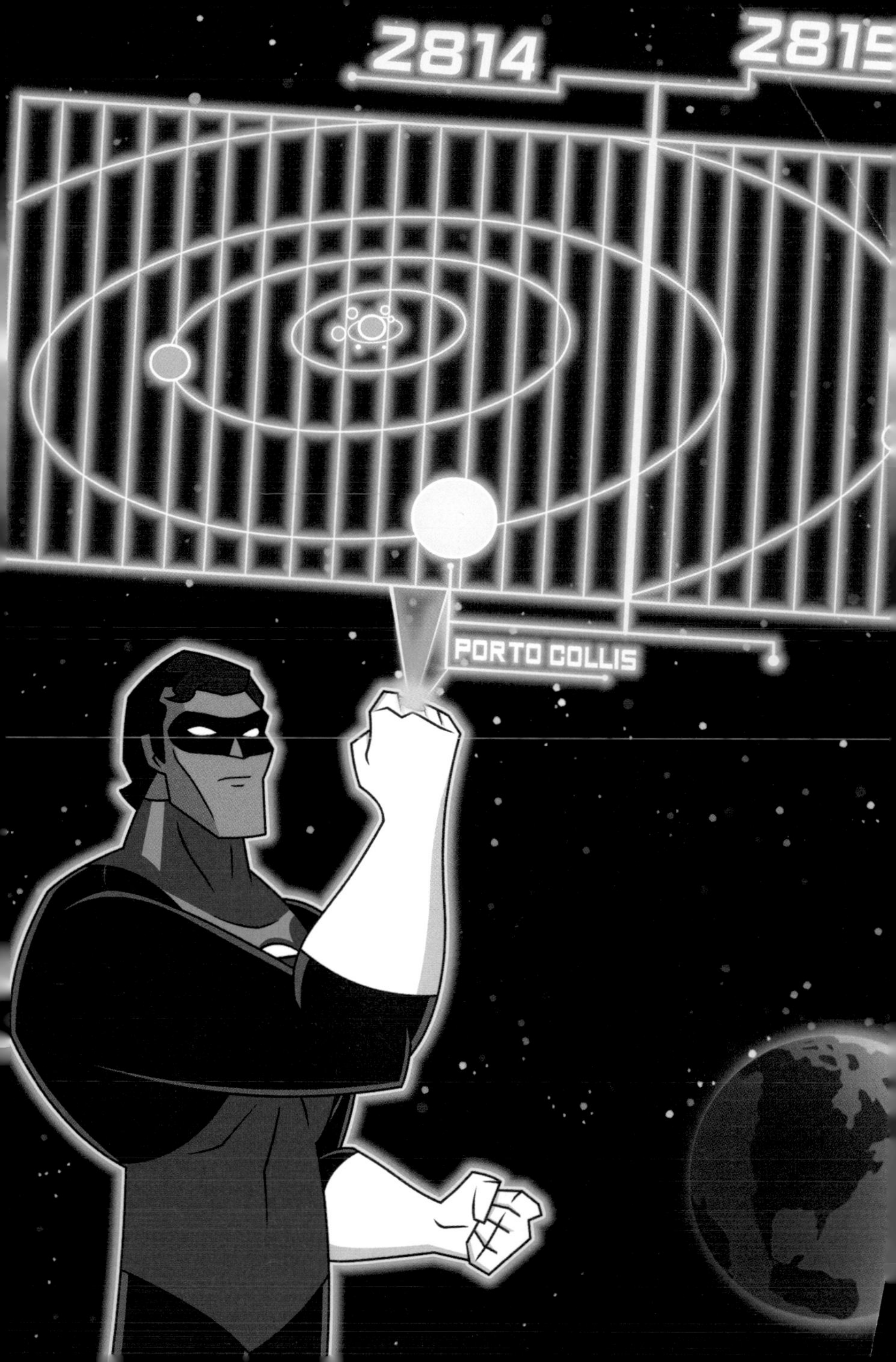
2814
2815
PORTO COLLIS

CHAPTER 2

STAR POWER!

As Hal approached Porto Collis, he saw that the small planet was very close to its sun. "Warning!" chimed his ring. "The current temperature is 1,811 degrees."

Hal didn't feel it. His ring protected him from the extreme cold of space — as well as the extreme heat on the surface. Hal saw that Porto Collis was entirely covered with silver-white seas. "All I see are oceans," said Hal. "Where's the platinum?"

"The oceans *are* the platinum," his ring informed him.

"The planet is currently so close to its sun," the ring added, "that it is hot enough to melt platinum into a liquid."

Hal was impressed. An entire planet covered with liquid platinum oceans!

"Porto Collis is continuing its orbital path," the ring went on. "It is moving away from its sun. The temperature is dropping quickly. Soon, the platinum will solidify."

ZZHAPPPPPPP! A beam of black light hit Hal in the back and sent him tumbling.

Hal smacked into a chunk of hardening platinum. Another beam of solid black light held Hal down. The platinum froze around his legs.

Hal looked up and saw the man in the star-shaped mask. "Your ring creates things out of solid green light," said the man.

He pointed to the metal band on his arm that was aimed right at Hal. "My Star-band uses solid black light the same way," the man said.

A beam of black light shot out and created a chair on the ground. The man sat down in it. "With your legs trapped, I could destroy you easily. But before I do, would you mind if we talked a little?" he asked. "My Star-band gets power from starlight, so I spend most of my time in deep space. Just between you and me, being out here with no one to talk to can drive a guy a crazy!"

"I can see that," said Hal. He hid his ring behind his back. The man in the star mask couldn't see that Hal was using it to create a small green jackhammer.

"I call myself Evil Star," said the man. "It's a scary name, don't you think?"

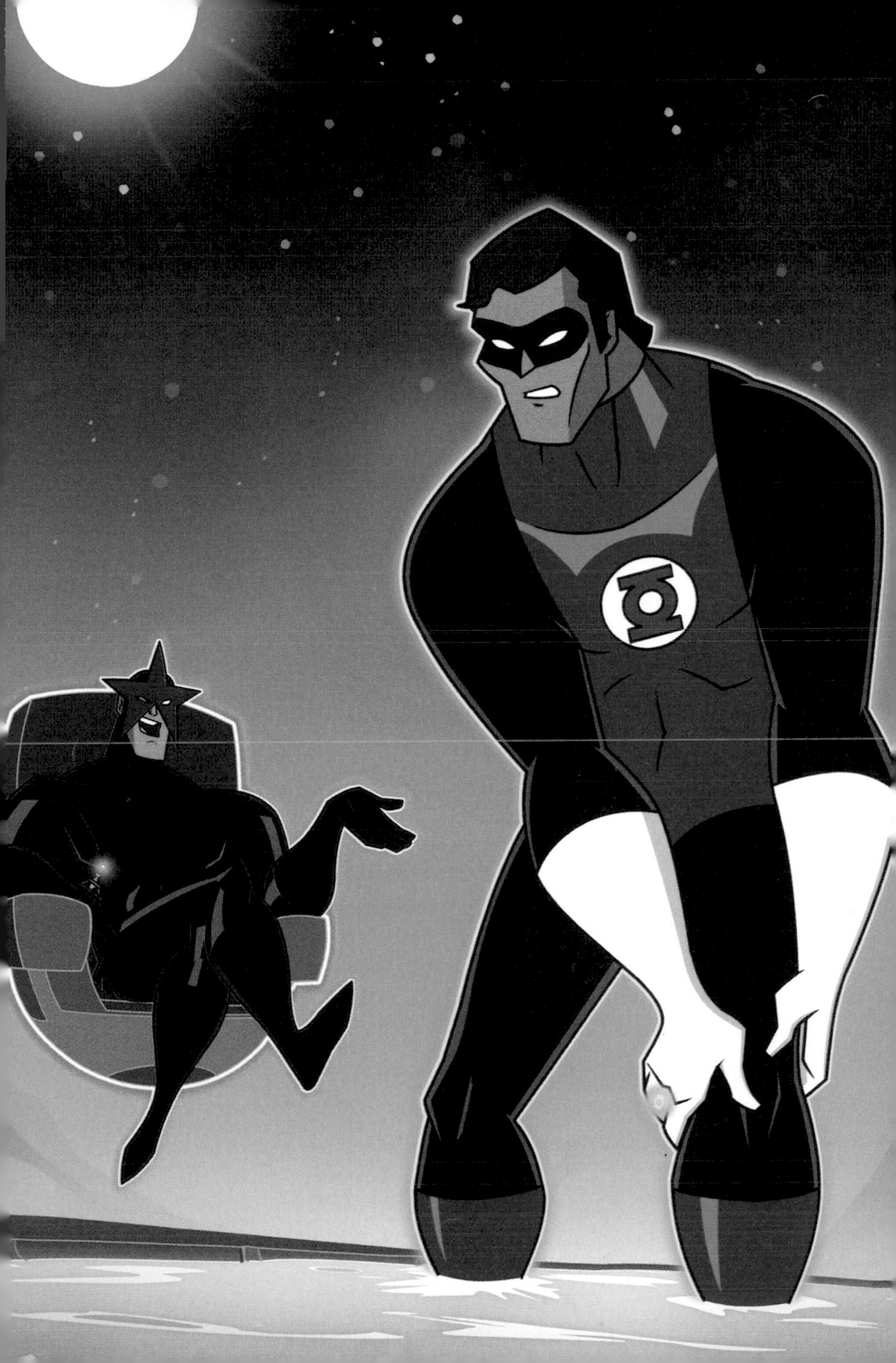

"Oh, yeah, real scary," said Hal. His green jackhammer silently dug through the metal that held Hal's legs.

"Thank you!" Evil Star said.

"No, thank *you*," said Hal as he pulled his legs out of the platinum, "for giving me time to break free!"

Evil Star pointed at something behind the Green Lantern. Hal turned to look just as several small creatures jumped on him.

"Those are my Starlings," said Evil Star.

Hal saw twelve identical Starlings. Each one was three feet tall. They looked like miniature versions of Evil Star. Hal's ring created a hammer, and he swung it at the Starlings. It hit one right in the chest. But instead of knocking the Starling aside, the hammer just fizzled away!

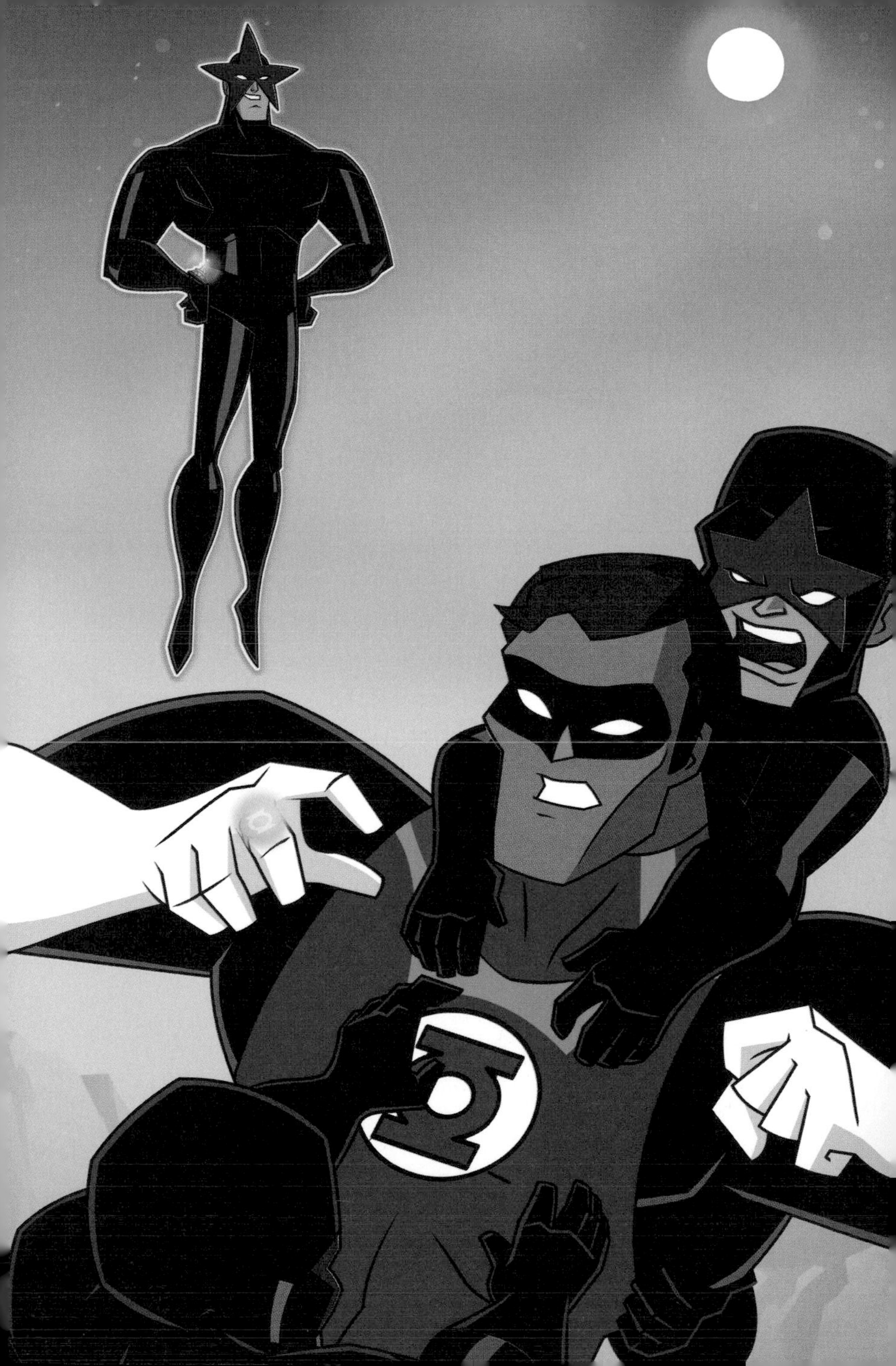

"The Starlings are made out of solid light," said Evil Star. "For some reason, they dissolve other things made out of light — like whatever your ring creates."

Hal struggled, but the little imps held him down. Together they were very strong. "As you can see, my Starlings are useful," said Evil Star. "However, they can't talk. And even if they could, they'd just agree with everything I said."

The Starlings all nodded in agreement.

"See? They have no minds of their own," Evil Star complained. "That makes them very boring. That's why I was excited to chat with you. But it seems our conversation is now over."

Evil Star raised his fist and pointed his deadly Star-band right at Hal.

CHAPTER 3

HELP ALMOST ARRIVES

"Stop!" boomed a voice from above.

"Who is that?" cried Evil Star, looking up for the source. The Starlings immediately let Hal go and flew up to find out.

"Wait! Don't let him go!" Evil Star screamed at his Starlings. "Get back here you mindless dolts!" Evil Star turned to ask Hal, "See what I have to deal with!?"

Hal wasn't there to answer. He had zipped out of sight behind a frozen wave of solid platinum.

Using his ring, Hal created a telescope. Through it, he saw the person who had told Evil Star to stop. Floating in space above Porto Collis was a female alien. On the alien's chest was the symbol of the Green Lantern Corps.

"Arisia!" said Hal, using his ring to communicate. "I'm glad you're here."

"Of course I'm here," replied the other Green Lantern through her ring. "I'm the Green Lantern of Sector 2815."

Thousands of Green Lanterns existed throughout the galaxy, each in their own sectors. Even though Sector 2815 was right next to Hal's sector, Hal rarely met with Arisia. The Green Lanterns had a rule — stay in your own sector.

"Do you remember me?" asked Hal.

"How could I forget?" replied Arisia. "Besides, I had my ring download your file when I saw you. I'm surprised you didn't do the same. Regulation states that upon meeting, Green Lanterns should —"

A blast destroyed the wave in front of Hal. Evil Star had found him. Huge chunks of platinum rained down on him.

"I can't believe you snuck away from me to talk to that weirdo up there," whined Evil Star. "You know how desperate I am for conversation!"

Evil Star hurled blasts down on Hal. Hal's ring formed an umbrella. The blasts bounced off. *ZHKINNGG!* "That 'weirdo' is another Green Lantern!" said Hal. "You don't stand a chance against both of us!"

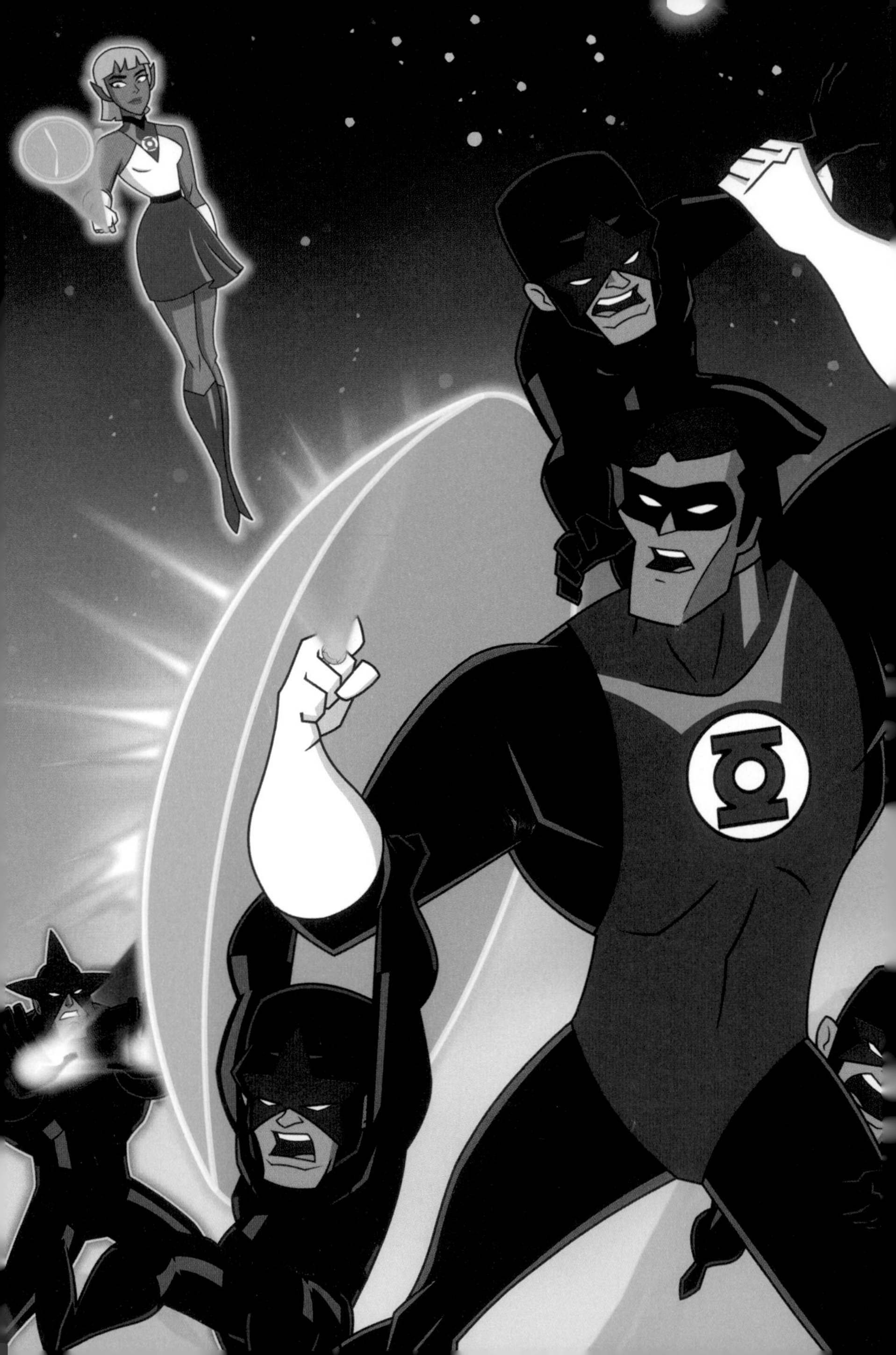

"That is true," agreed Arisia as she floated above. "Together, Hal Jordan and I would have no trouble stopping you." But Arisia wasn't doing anything to stop Evil Star. She just floated above the planet while Evil Star continued to attack Hal.

"Um, any time you want to help," Hal called up to her.

"In a minute," replied Arisia.

BANG! Evil Star blasted Hal to the ground. "Why not right now?" Hal shouted.

"That's against the rules," said Arisia.

"What are talking about?" Hal cried as he dodged another blast from Evil Star.

"Porto Collis is in your sector right now," Arisia explained. "The Book of Oa clearly states that Green Lanterns are supposed to stay in their own sectors."

"I am on the border between our two sectors," Arisia said. "Until Porto Collis reaches this point in its orbit, there is nothing I can do to help."

Down on the planet, Hal zoomed away from Evil Star. He managed to lose the villain in a maze of platinum mountains, only to find the Starlings in his way!

"Of course there's something you can do!" Hal yelled, backing away from the Starlings. "You can break the rules!"

"No, I cannot," replied Arisia. "I knew one day I might be tempted to, so I programmed my ring to turn itself off whenever I entered another sector."

Hal watched the twelve Starlings climb onto each other. Their bodies fused together as they merged into a single, giant Starling.

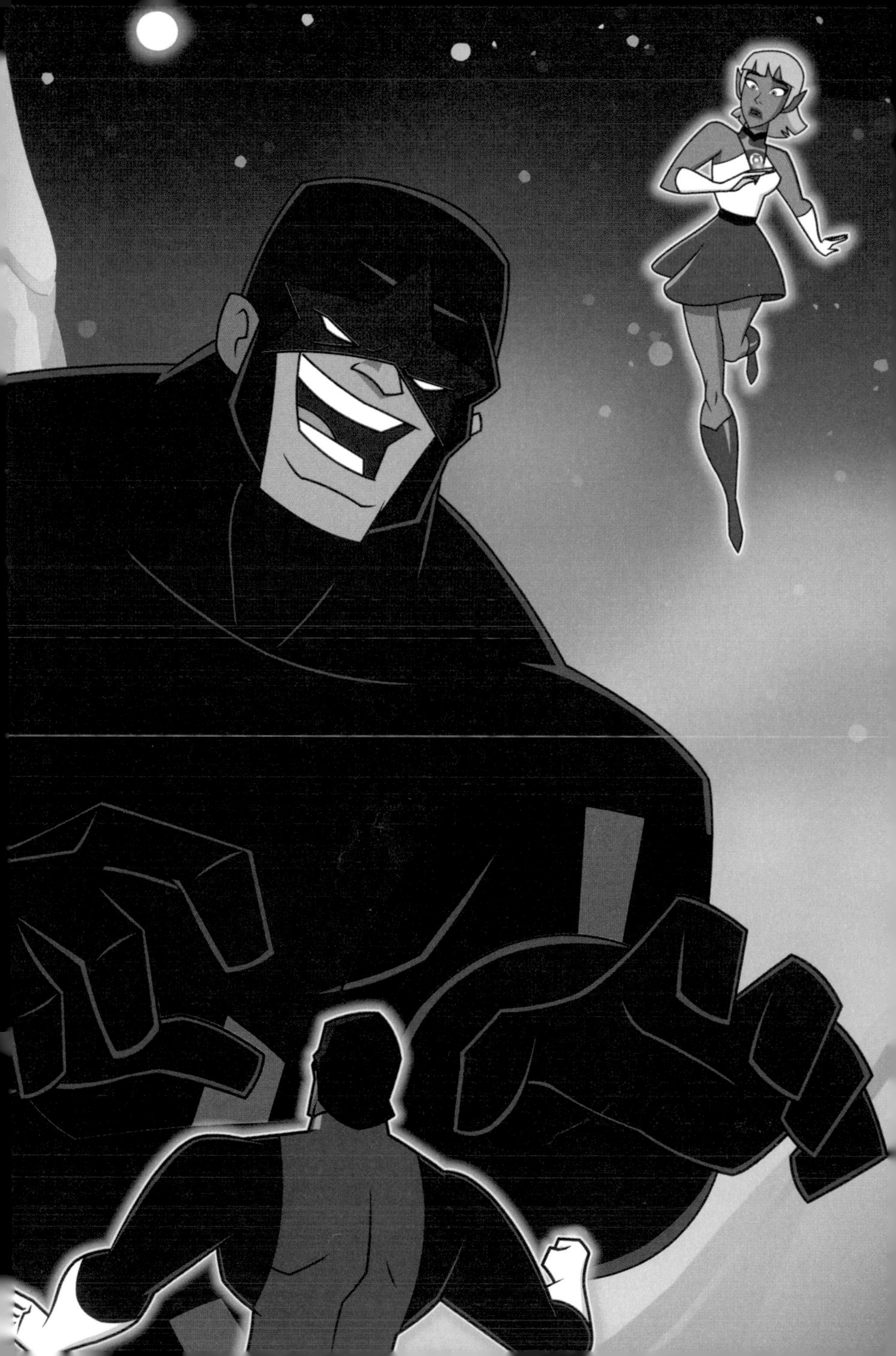

SMASH! The giant stomped over the frozen platinum toward Hal.

"Fear not, Hal Jordan," said Arisia from above. "Porto Collis will be between our sectors in sixty seconds."

Sixty seconds?! thought Hal. *I'll be lucky to make it through the next ten!*

Hal aimed his ring at the hulking Starling. **BOOM!** A shiny green missile blasted the Starling right in the belly.

Hal smiled . . . until he saw the missile just fizzle away when it hit the Starling. It didn't hurt the creature at all.

The giant Starling swung a fist the size of a car. **THWACK!** It knocked Hal to the ground and held him there. The Starling pushed down on Hal. He was slowly being crushed.

CHAPTER 4

A BIG PROBLEM

Suddenly, something grabbed Hal and pulled him free. It was Arisia!

"Oh, so *now* you're ready to help?" asked Hal, annoyed. "Thanks, but I think I'll take my chances on my own."

"No you won't," said Arisia.

"What?" Hal shouted.

"It's a regulation in the Book of Oa," said Arisia. "Porto Collis is now on the border. Technically, it's in *both* of our sectors. We have to work together."

"Wait a minute," said Hal. "Do you have all the rules and regulations in the Book of Oa memorized?"

"All the updates, too," said Arisia proudly. "I get them downloaded right to my ring. You really should as well. That's what the Guardians say all Green Lanterns should do . . ."

RUMMMMMMMBLE! The ground shook under Hal and Arisia's feet. The two Green Lanterns turned to see the giant Starling stomp toward them.

"Right now," said Hal, "I say rule number one is to stop that thing!"

"That just shows how much you don't know," said Arisia. "Rule number one is always check that your ring is properly charged every 24 hours —"

WHAM! The giant Starling slammed Arisia to the ground before she could finish the thought.

Hal pulled Arisia aside as the giant Starling threw another punch.

"Our rings are no good against that thing," said Hal. "Somehow, the Starlings are able to dissolve anything we build."

"The Book of Oa tells stories of other Green Lanterns who have fought similar creatures," said Arisia. "The solution is simple. Don't hit it with your ring."

Arisia held out her hand. Her ring glowed brightly and created a catapult that was almost as big as the giant itself.

"Use your ring to hit it with something else!" she said. The Starling charged at the two Green Lanterns.

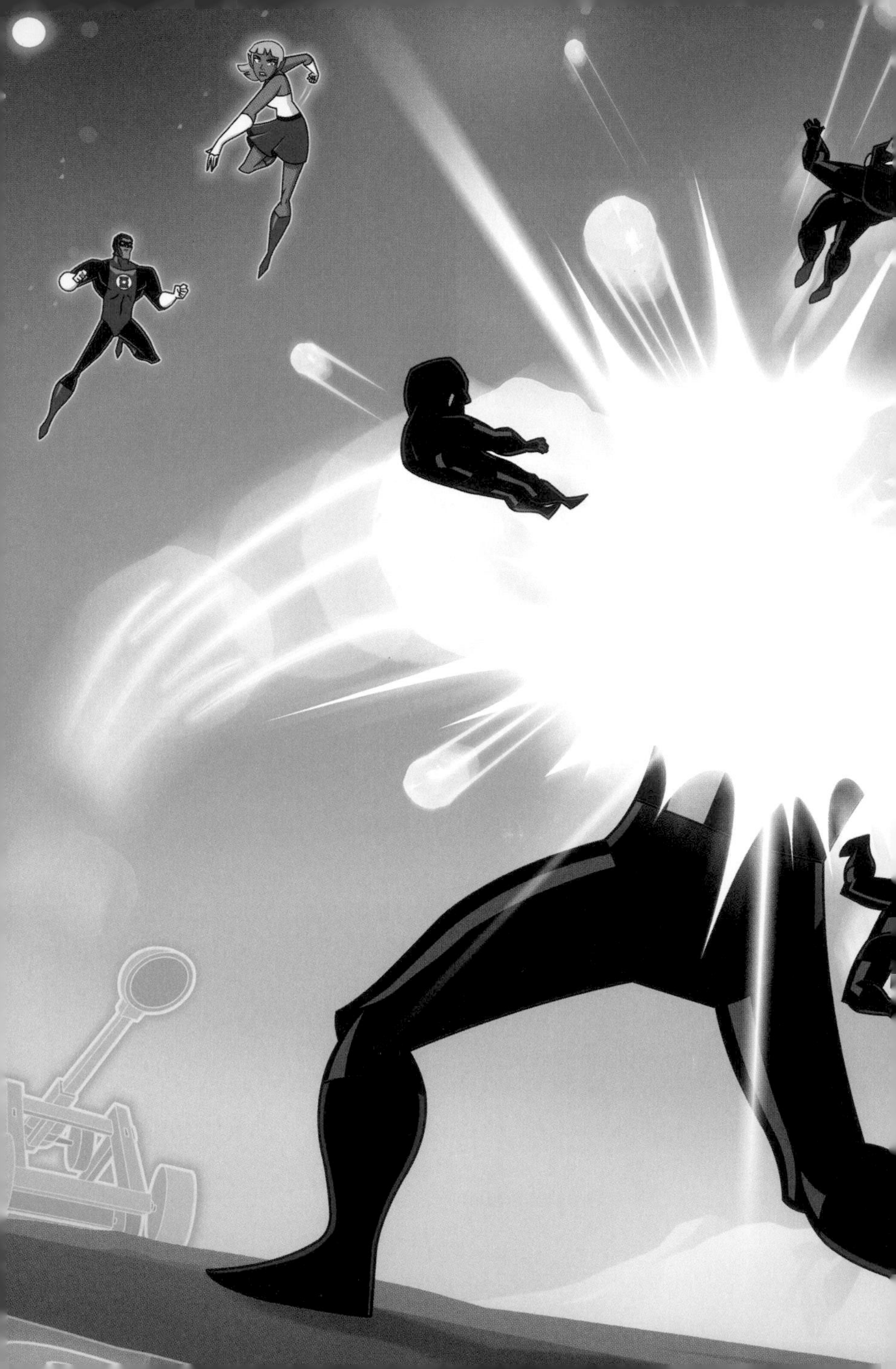

Arisia's catapult scooped up a chunk of solid platinum the size of a house. The catapult threw the metal boulder right into the Starling's chest.

KRAK! The boulder hit the Starling and broke into a dozen pieces. So did the enormous Starling. The giant crumpled and separated back into the dozen tiny Starlings that had formed it.

Hal was impressed. "I guess knowing every last word in the Book of Oa has its advantages," he said.

"Our rules and regulations are not meant to hold us back," said Arisia. "They are what allow us to succeed."

Arisia used her ring to scoop up another hunk of platinum. The ring bent the metal into a cage.

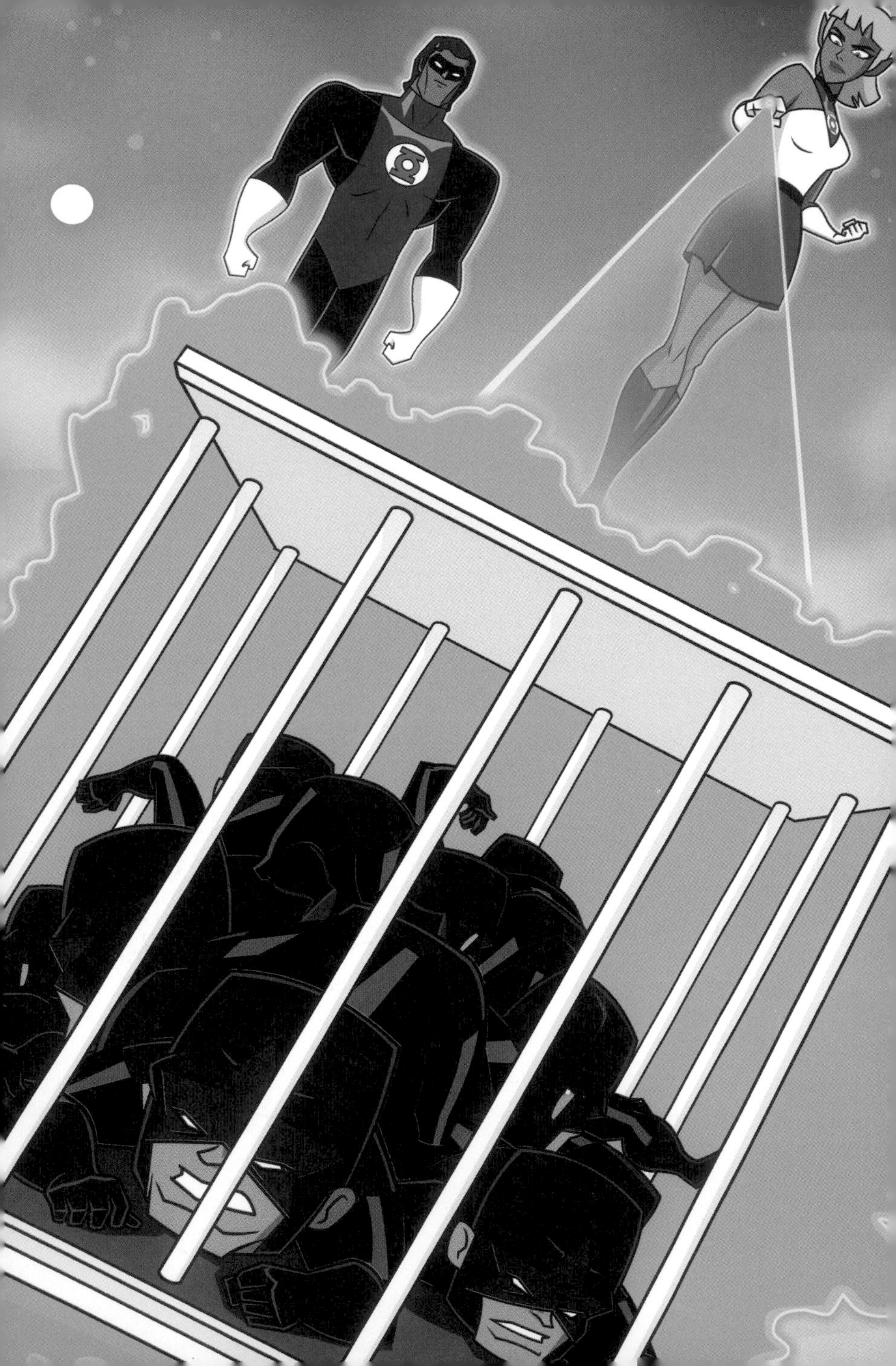

Arisia slammed the silver cage on top of the Starlings, trapping them inside. Then she hurled the cage into space.

"We can pick them up after we catch Evil Star," Arisia said.

Hal pointed to the horizon at Evil Star. The thief was using his Star-band to dig into a mountain of platinum so he could steal it. "Is there anything in the Book of Oa about how to deal with a guy like him?" Hal asked.

Arisia nodded. "This situation calls for the Medphyll Maneuver," said Arisia. She pointed to the mountain of platinum. "Go to the top of that mountain. Wait for my signal."

Hal flew off. Then he stopped. "What's a 'Medphyll Maneuver?'" he asked.

He turned toward Arisia, and saw that she was in trouble. As Arisia flew at Evil Star, the villain blasted the Green Lantern out of the sky.

Hal raced toward them. With his ring, Hal created a big green bat that bashed Evil Star aside. At the same time, Hal made a giant catcher's mitt and caught Arisia just before she hit the ground.

"You're welcome," Hal said with a smile.

"Why would I thank you?" cried Arisia. "You just ruined everything!"

"What are you talking about?" replied Hal. "Evil Star had you on the ropes."

"I was not in trouble. I just wanted Evil Star to think I was. That's what the Medphyll Maneuver is all about!" said Arisia.

"You know," said Hal, "you're not the easiest partner to work with."

"You're complaining?" shouted Arisia. "*You're* the one who doesn't know the Book of Oa. You're doing everything wrong!"

Before Hal could answer, Arisia's ring chirped out an alert. "Attention," said the ring, "This planet has now moved entirely into Sector —"

The ring was interrupted. Evil Star fired blast after blast as he flew back over the mountain.

KA-BOOM! The mountain shook as Evil Star's blasts tore the top off of it. As 10,000 tons of platinum fell toward the Green Lanterns, a giant fist flew out of Hal's ring.

The big green fist smashed the metal into a thousand harmless pieces. Then, the fist slammed into Evil Star. He fell backward, tumbling head over feet. Evil Star crashed into the ground a mile away.

Hal raced toward him. "Wait!" cried Arisia. Her ring created a giant pair of pincers that grabbed Hal and held him up.

"What are you doing?" cried Hal. "Evil Star is down. We can catch him!"

"No," said Arisia evenly. "*We* can't."

"Porto Collis has continued its orbit around its sun," stated Arisia's ring. "This planet is now entirely in Sector 2815, so that regulation no longer applies."

"A Green Lantern is supposed to protect her own sector," said Arisia. "Hers and only hers. This is my sector — not yours."

Hal couldn't believe it. "If you're going to stick to the rules instead of letting me help, then you're just as crazy as Evil Star!" he said.

"Sticking to the rules is what allows us to succeed," replied Arisia.

"Warning!" Hal's ring called out. "Power levels at zero percent. Flight capability also at zero percent."

"What's going on?" Hal asked his ring.

Arisia answered instead. "I told you before that I had programmed my ring to turn itself off if I ever entered another Green Lantern's sector," she said. "It is also programmed to turn off other Green Lanterns' rings if they enter *my* sector."

"I didn't know the rings could do that!" exclaimed Hal.

"That does not surprise me," said Arisia. She then used her ring to create a glowing green rocket ship. "As long as you are inside my space sector, you will not be able to use your ring. Take this rocket back to your sector. I will handle Evil Star."

Arisia didn't wait for a reply. She flew into the air and raced after Evil Star alone.

"Wait!" cried Hal. Hal jumped up to fly after her — and fell to the ground.

THUD!

"Power levels at zero percent," his ring reminded him.

Hal sighed. Because Arisia was sticking to the rules, Hal had no choice. There was only one thing he could do.

He climbed inside the green rocket.

CHAPTER 5

BATTLE IN SECTOR 2815

As Porto Collis drifted farther into Sector 2815, the skies grew dark. Now that the planet was far from its sun, the only light came from the stars. That made Evil Star smile. "Starlight is what gives me my strength!" he said.

BANG! BANG! Evil Star fired away. Arisia's ring created a shield, but the force of the Star-band's blasts sent her crashing to the ground.

Arisia knew every trick in the Book of Oa. As she fought Evil Star, she used tactics that had won a thousand battles before.

Nothing worked. Bathed in the starlight that gave him his strength, Evil Star was too powerful.

Suddenly, a green rocket flew right at Evil Star. It was Hal! As the rocket crashed into the villain, Hal jumped clear. The rocket exploded in a fiery ball of smoke and flames. **WHOOOOSH!**

A few yards away, Hal struggled to his feet. "Warning," Hal's ring stated. "Power levels are at zero percent."

"Do you have any good news to tell me for a change?" Hal asked his ring.

The ring was silent. "Figures," Hal said.

"What are you doing here?" Arisia cried as she flew to Hal's side.

"If that's your way of saying, 'thanks,'" said Hal, "then you're welcome."

"You are breaking an important Green Lantern regulation!" said Arisia.

"Enough!" a voice howled. Hal and Arisia turned and saw Evil Star emerge from the smoke and fire. "There's too much starlight now for a little explosion like that to harm me," the villain said. "But your arguing is really starting to hurt my ears!"

"So if you don't mind," he added, "I'm just going to go ahead and steal the platinum — and get rid of you two for good."

Evil Star used his Star-band to create two monstrous mining machines. Each machine was a hundred feet tall with enormous digging arms. The thief hopped into one of the crab-like machines and stomped off, scooping up platinum as he went.

The other machine swung its pincer arms at Arisia and Hal. Arisia leaped into the air and out of the way. Without his ring's powers, Hal couldn't fly. All he could do was jump. CRUNCH! The giant crab missed him by an inch.

"Turn on my ring!" Hal yelled at Arisia.

"I can't!" protested Arisia as she battled the giant mining machine.

"Come on!" Hal couldn't believe it. "Just this once, couldn't you *bend* the rules?"

"Even if I could," Arisia said, "we can't stop Evil Star. I've tried everything in the Book of Oa against him! Nothing worked."

"Then we'll have to try something that's not in the book," said Hal, "I have an idea. But since my ring isn't working, you'll have to use yours."

Hal told Arisia his plan. Arisia's eyes went wide. "Is that even possible?" she asked. "There's nothing in the Book of Oa about any Green Lantern doing anything like that before."

"There's nothing in the book about Evil Star either," replied Hal. "No Green Lantern has ever fought him before. When you're facing something new, sometimes you have to make things up as you go."

"Make things up as you go . . . ?" repeated Arisia. In her time as a Green Lantern, that was one thing she had never done.

"Don't worry," smiled Hal. "I do it all the time."

Arisia sighed. She had no choice but to hope Hal's plan worked.

Arisia lit up her ring and created a green hand. The hand grew and grew and grew. Soon it was the size of an elephant. Then it was as big as an airplane.

Arisia started to sweat as she forced the hand to get bigger and bigger. It seconds, it was as big as the planet Porto Collis itself!

"Warning!" chimed Arisia's ring. "You are currently using 100% of your ring's power reserves."

"That means we are unable to defend ourselves," said Arisia. "This is completely against the regulations!"

"Evil Star doesn't play by the rules!" yelled Hal. "So, if we're going to stop him, then neither can we."

Arisia nodded. She willed the giant green hand to grab hold of the planet.

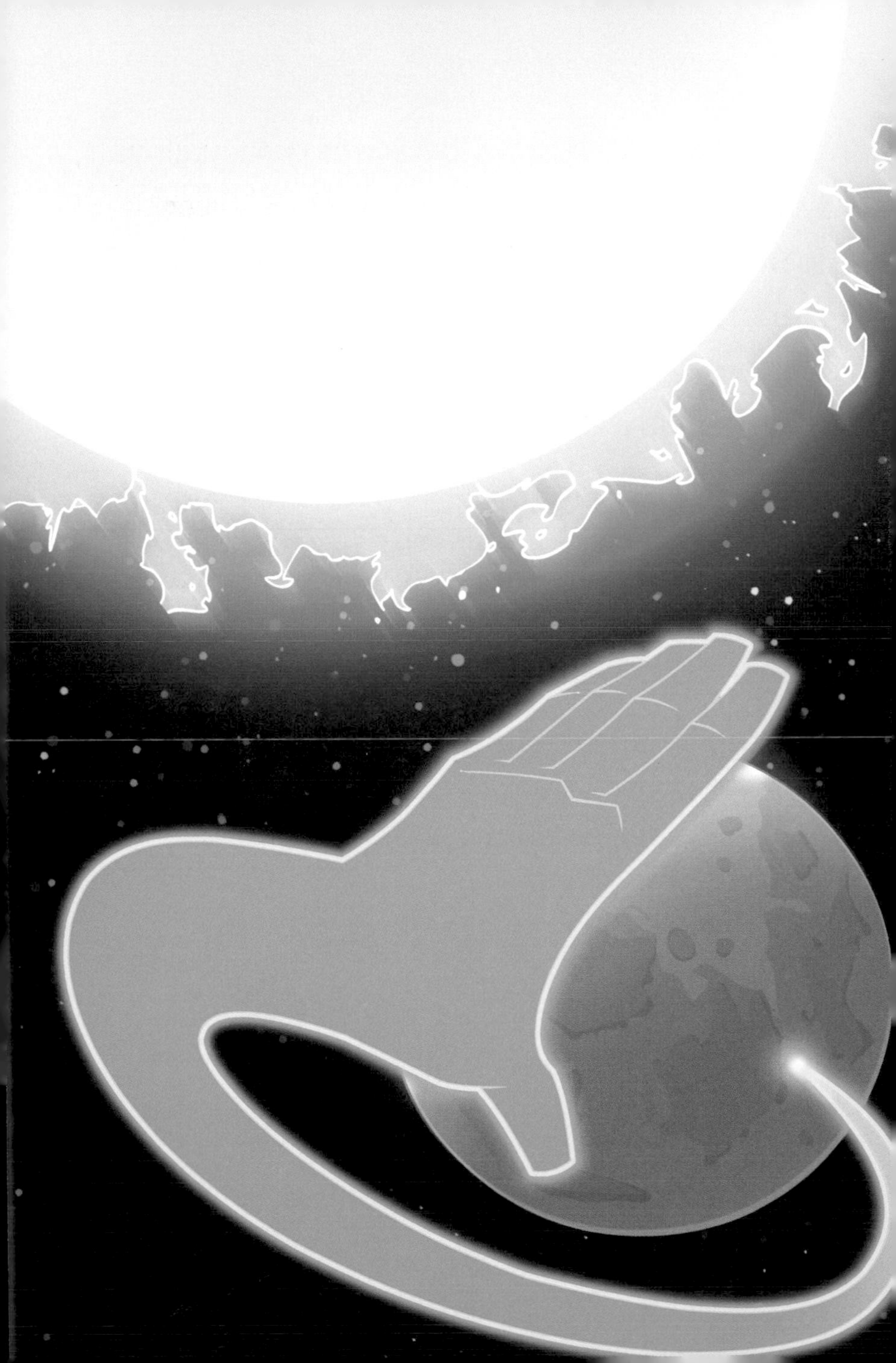

At the same time, the giant crab-like machine stomped toward them. Hal waved his arms wildly, trying to draw it away from Arisia. Its giant crab-arm rushed down toward her. Hal ducked, and the arm slashed just over his head.

WHOOOOSH!

Hal turned to run, but his foot tripped on a large chunk of platinum. The giant arm swung back at him. There was nowhere to escape. The thousand-ton arm landed right on top of him . . . and bounced off!

"Defensive power levels at 100%," his ring said. Hal's ring was working again.

Arisia had done it! She had pushed the planet back to the border between the two sectors. Hal's plan had worked.

Using both their rings, the two Green Lanterns easily tore apart the machine that had been attacking them. Then they went after Evil Star.

Now that the planet was once again close to its sun, the platinum was starting to melt. They found Evil Star in his mining machine, stuck in the molten metal. With the sun so close, hardly any starlight could be seen in the sky. Evil Star was now no match for the two Green Lanterns.

Hal and Arisia both pointed their rings at the frightened villain. As their rings glowed with green power, the two super heroes looked at each other and smiled.

"Beware *our* power!" they shouted together, blasting their rings toward Evil Star. THUOOOOMMMMMM!!

Within seconds, the defeated villain sat scowling inside a glowing green cage. Hal turned to Arisia.

"We may not have done it by the book," Hal said with a smile, "but we found a way to stop Evil Star. That's something no Green Lantern has ever done before."

"There is still the matter of the rules," Arisia said. "The next time you enter my sector . . ." Arisia paused. Then she laughed, "I will be very happy to see you!"

Hal couldn't believe it. He had gotten Arisia to laugh about breaking the rules.

Hal couldn't help but smile. For the third time today, he had done something no one else had ever done before.

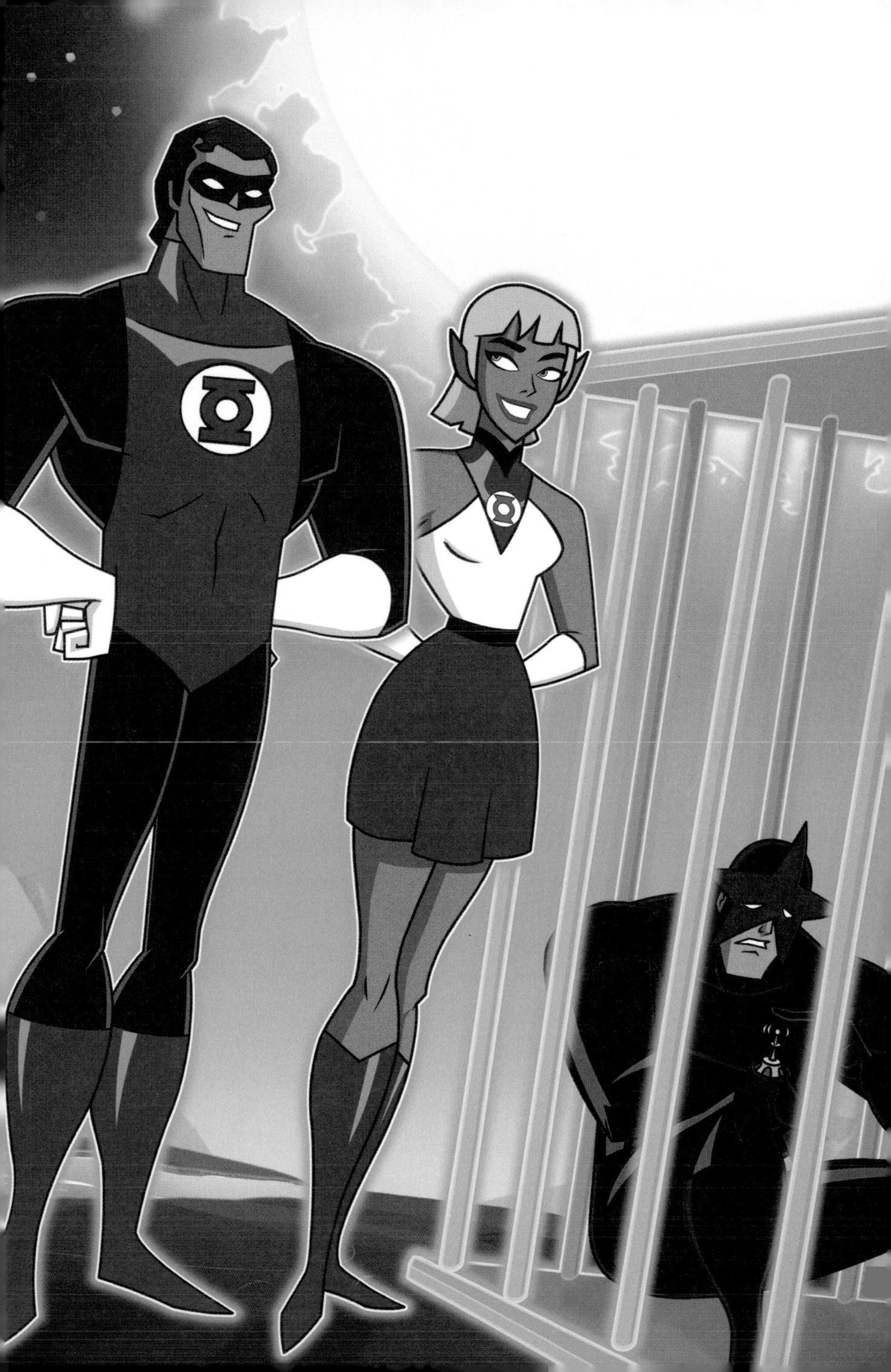

EVIL STAR

BIRTHPLACE: Aoran

OCCUPATION: Space criminal

HEIGHT: 6' 1"   **WEIGHT:** 205 lbs.

EYES: Blue   **HAIR:** Blonde

POWERS/ABILITIES: Brilliant scientist; highly intellectual; Star-band weapon allows flight, hard-light constructs, prolonged life; able to command mini Starlings.

BIOGRAPHY

As a scientist on the planet Aoran, Evil Star studied immortality, or the ability to live forever. Soon, he invented the Star-band, a weapon that drains energy from the stars and gives its user eternal life. With this powerful tool, Evil Star conquered his home planet and then looked for new worlds to take over. He is not alone in this quest. Several miniature versions of the villain, called Starlings, follow their master's every command. They will stop at nothing to fulfill his destiny — to become the most powerful villain of all.

Before leaving Aoran, Evil Star wiped out the entire population of his home planet with his powerful Star-band weapon.

Evil Star's Star-band is similar to a Green Lantern's power ring. The weapon can create hard-light constructs from anything the user can imagine. However, without starlight, the Star-band cannot function and its powers quickly fade away.

Unlike power rings, the Star-band is a weapon of pure evil. The deadly device causes its user to crave dark powers.

With his Star-band, Evil Star created tiny versions of himself called Starlings. These mini men are mindless and obey Evil Star's every command.

BIOGRAPHIES

Scott Sonneborn has written 20 books, one circus (for Ringling Bros. Barnum & Bailey), and a bunch of TV shows. He's been nominated for one Emmy and spent three very cool years working at DC Comics. He lives in Los Angeles with his wife and their two sons.

Dan Schoening was born in Victoria, B.C., Canada. From an early age, Dan has had a passion for animation and comic books. Currently, Dan does freelance work in the animation and game industry and spends a lot of time with his lovely little daughter, Paige.

GLOSSARY

catapult (KAT-uh-puhlt)—a weapon, similar to a large slingshot, used for firing rocks or other objects

cockpit (KOK-pit)—the front section of a plane where the pilot sits

corps (KOR)—a group of people acting together

galaxy (GAL-uhk-see)—a very large group of stars and planets

guardian (GAR-dee-uhn)—someone who guards or protects something

hangar (HANG-ur)—a large building where aircrafts are kept

maneuver (muh-NOO-ver)—a difficult movement that needs planning and skill

platinum (PLAT-uhn-uhm)—a valuable silvery-white metal that is often used in jewelry

regulation (reg-yuh-LAY-shuhn)—an official rule or order

tactics (TAK-tiks)—plans or methods to win a battle

DISCUSSION QUESTIONS

1. Even though Hal Jordan needed help, Arisia refused to break the rules. Is breaking the rules ever okay? Why or why not?

2. Evil Star's weapon, the Star-band, makes the villain uncontrollably mean. Do you think he should be blamed for his actions? Explain.

3. Green Lanterns have green power rings. If you could choose any color to give you power, what would it be? Why?

WRITING PROMPTS

1. Even Green Lanterns must obey some rules. Write a list of rules that you follow each day. How do they help you? Have you ever broken one of them?

2. If you could travel to any planet in the solar system, where would you go? Write about where you would travel and why.

3. Evil Star gets his superpowers from the stars. Create your own villain or super hero that gets powers from outer space. Describe what your villain or hero looks like. What adventures do they have?

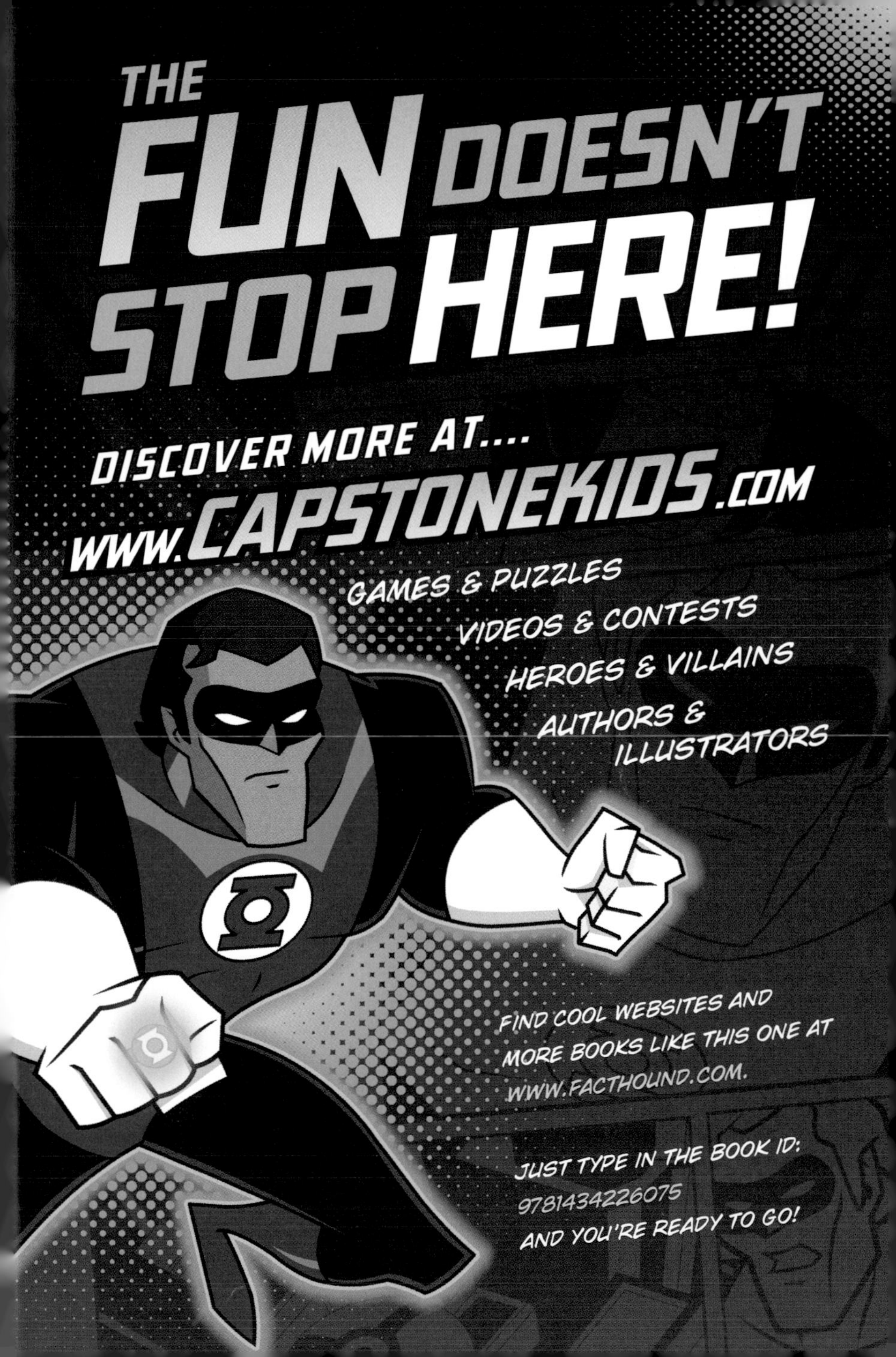
THE
FUN DOESN'T
STOP HERE!
DISCOVER MORE AT....
WWW.CAPSTONEKIDS.COM
GAMES & PUZZLES
VIDEOS & CONTESTS
HEROES & VILLAINS
AUTHORS & ILLUSTRATORS
FIND COOL WEBSITES AND MORE BOOKS LIKE THIS ONE AT WWW.FACTHOUND.COM.
JUST TYPE IN THE BOOK ID:
9781434226075
AND YOU'RE READY TO GO!

MORE NEW
GREEN LANTERN
ADVENTURES!

THE LAST SUPER HERO

BATTLE OF THE BLUE LANTERNS

THE LIGHT KING STRIKES!

HIGH-TECH TERROR

GUARDIAN OF EARTH

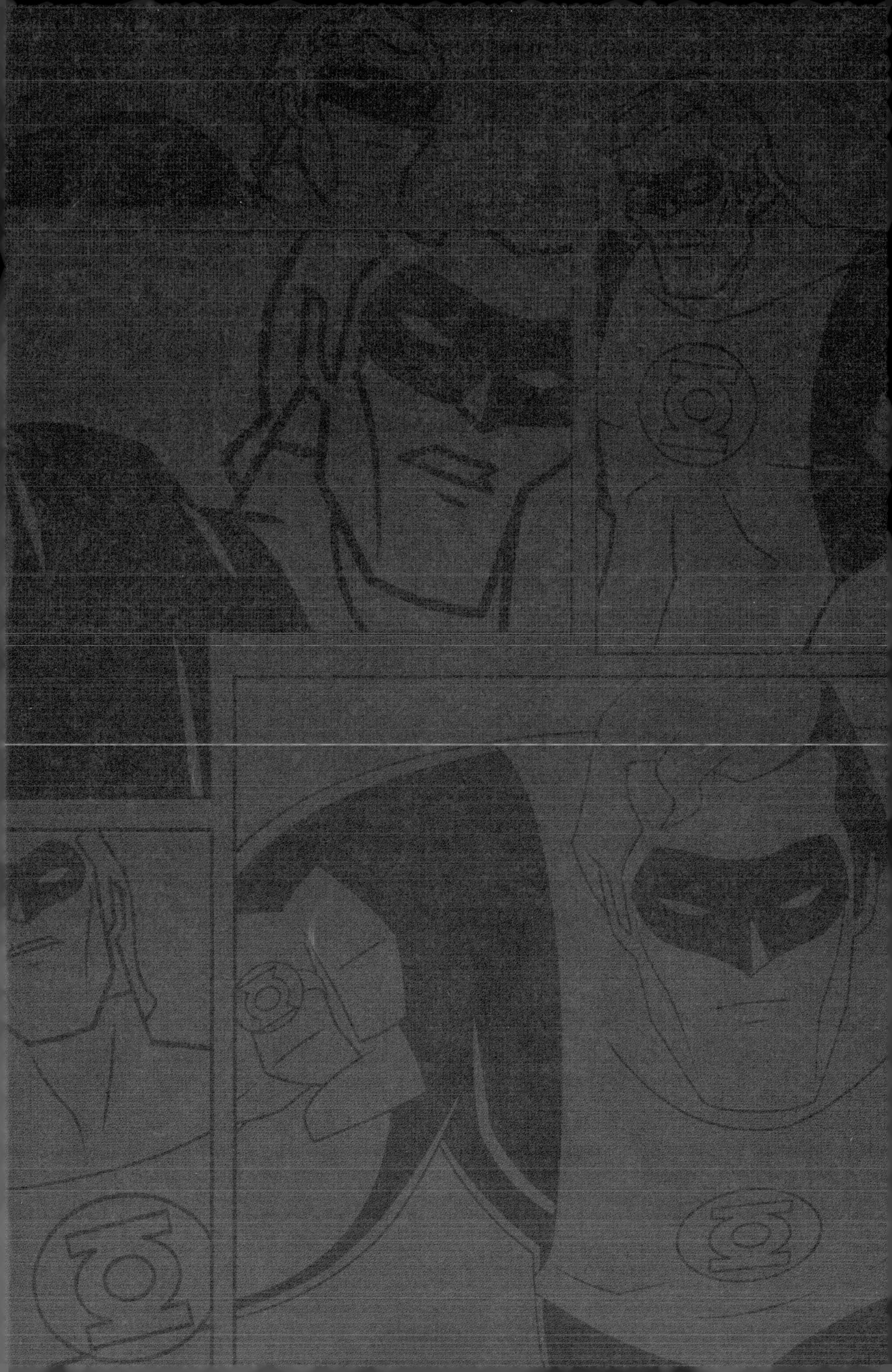

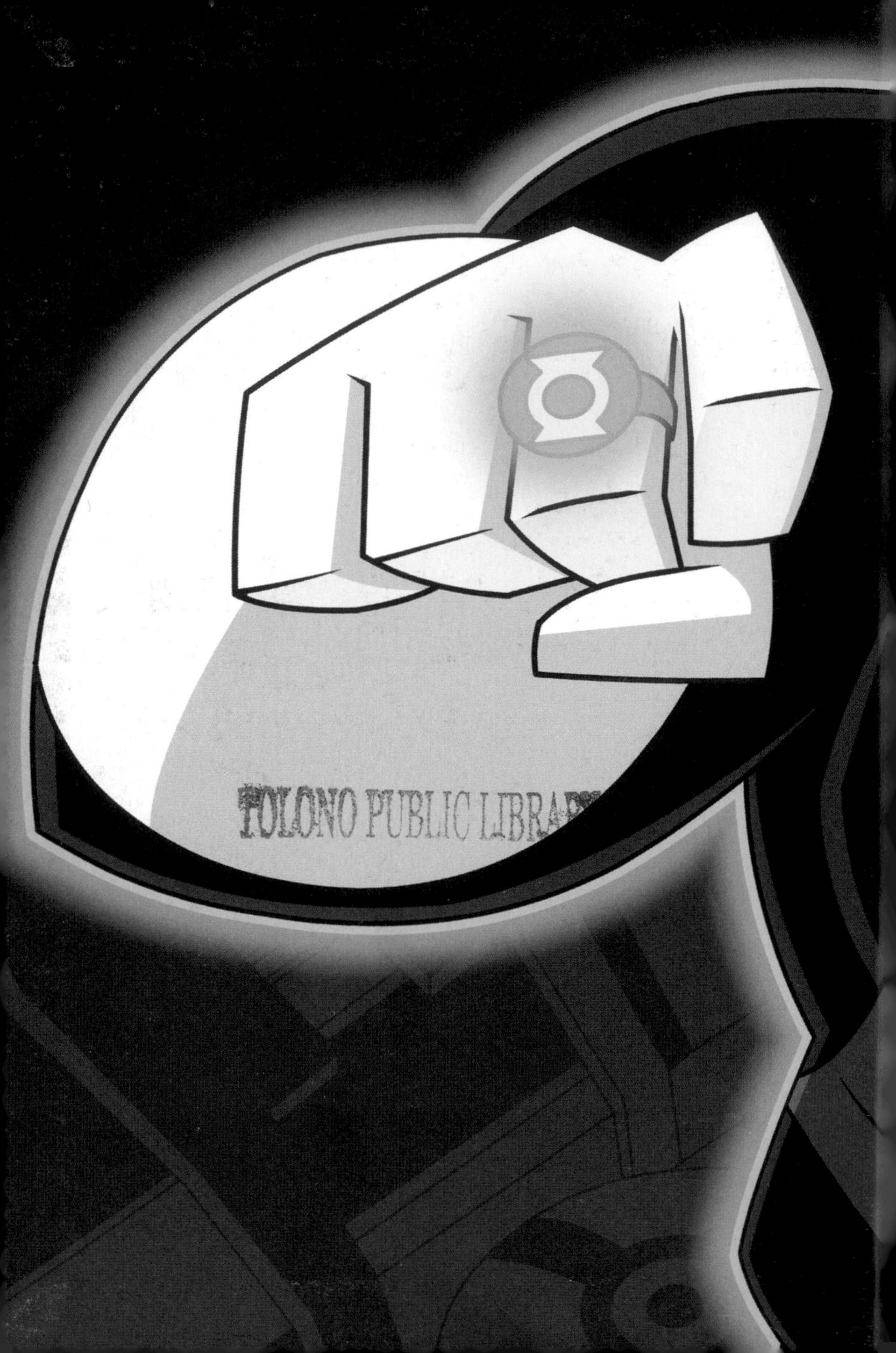